CELEBRATE STORIES. LOVE READING.

This book has been specially written, illustrated and published to celebrate **World Book Day**. We are a charity who offers every child and young person the opportunity to read and love books by giving you the chance to have a book of your own. To find out more, and for oodles of fun activities and reading recommendations to continue your reading journey, visit **worldbookday.com**.

World Book Day in the UK and Ireland is made possible by generous sponsorship from National Book Tokens, participating publishers, booksellers, authors and illustrators. The £1* book tokens are a gift from your local bookseller.

World Book Day works in partnership with a number of charities, all of whom are working to encourage a love of reading for pleasure.

The National Literacy Tr dren and young people to enjoy rea ke a big difference to how well yo e in life.

The Reading Agency ead for pleasure and empowerme artnership with libraries; they also support reading groups in schools and libraries all year round. Find out more and join your local library. summerreadingchallenge.org.uk

World Book Day also facilitates fundraising for:

Book Aid International, an international book donation and library development charity. Every year, they provide one million books to libraries and schools in communities where children would otherwise have little or no opportunity to read. bookaid.org

Read for Good, who motivate children in schools to read for fun through its sponsored read, which thousands of schools run on World Book Day and throughout the year. The money raised provides new books and resident storytellers in all the children's hospitals in the UK. readforgood.org

*€1.50 in Ireland

FOR DAVID, GEORGE AND CARRIE

First published 2019
by The O'Brien Press Ltd,
12 Terenure Road East, Rathgar,
Dublin 6, D06 HD27, Ireland.

Tel: +353 1 4923333;
Fax: +353 1 4922777

Email: books@obrien.ie
Website: www.obrien.ie

The O'Brien Press is a member of Publishing Ireland.

ISBN: 978-1-78849-087-0

7 6 5 4 3 2 1
24 23 22 21 20 19

Editing: The O'Brien Press Limited

Printed and bound by CPI Group (UK) Ltd, Croydon, CR0 4YY.

The paper in this book is produced using pulp from managed forests.

Published in

DUBLIN
UNESCO
City of Literature

CHAPTER ONE
WINNER WINNER, SCONES FOR DINNER

BBRRRIIINNNNNNNNGGGGGGG,
BBRRRIIINNNNNNNNGGGGGGG.

BBRRRIIINNNNNNNNGGGGGGG,
BBRRRIIINNNNNNNNGGGGGGG.

BBRRRIIINNNNNNNNGGGGGGG, BBRRRII–

(Boop boop bip boop boop boop bip booop.)

BBRRRIIINNNNNNNNGGGGGGG,
BBRRRIIINNNNNNNNGGGGGGG.

BBRRRIIINNNNNNNNGGGGGGG,
BBRRRIIINNNNNNNNGGGGGGG.

BBRRRIIINNNNNNNNGGGGGGG,
BBRRRIIINNNNNNNNGGGGGGG.

BRRRII–

(Boop boop bip boop boop boop bip booooop.)

BBRRRIIINNNNNNNNGGGGGGG,
BBRRRIIINNNNNNNNGGGGGGG.

BBRRRIIINNNNNNNNGGGGGGG, BBRRRIIINNNNN–

Klik.

'Hi there! This is DJ Liz Anya, and you're through to
Clobberstown FM, broadcasting all over the Clobberstown, Clontipper
and Cairnbrook areas! You're live on air, so please no naughty noises
or R.U.D.E. rumblings!'

'I make no promises.'

'Sorry? What was that?'

'Nothing, please continue.'

'Oh-kay… So caller, what's your name and where do you come from?'

'Who wants to know?'

'Em, DJ Liz Anya?'

'Fair enough. The name's Gigg, Nanny Gigg, and I'm from Clobberstown.'

'So, Nanny Gigg from Clobberstown, we are looking for caller seventeen to be the winner of three tickets to see the FAB-U-LOUS Roaming Scones in the Showjump Arena on Friday night. The prize includes bed and breakfast in the *ultra*-posh Duck & Duvet B&B and a pre-show VIP meet and greet with the Roaming Scones rock stars themselves, the legendary Eddie and Pete! *Total* LEDGES!'

'Go on ... '

'Gigg, Nanny Gigg ... YOU ARE CALLER SEVENTEEN! YOU AND TWO FRIENDS ARE GOING TO SEE THE SCONES!!'

'Oh. My. DOG!!'

Nanny Gigg emitted a loud, piercing squeal, so high-pitched that several of the dogs and a couple of the llamas in the backyard started to howl. Sindy the budgie flapped off her usual perch on Gigg's shoulder in a cloud of turquoise feathers. Nanny Gigg shoved her mobile phone in her mouth and, bouncing high on her wrinkly toes, did a cartwheel across the kitchen. As she did so, one of her feet caught the handle of a metal saucepan and it crashed to the floor

7

with a loud KLANNNGGGG! which made Nanny Gigg whoop even louder.

All this ruckus drew the attention of her granddaughter Sam Hannigan, who was cleaning out the llama enclosure in the back garden with her best friend, Ajay Patel.

'Is your granny okay?' asked Ajay, looking in through the kitchen window of Clobberstown Lodge. All he could see was a pair of pink-slippered feet waving wildly around behind the glass.

'That's the big question, all right,' said Sam, brushing her curly red hair out of her eyes. 'Now, give me a hand with this hay bale.'

'Hello? Nanny Gigg? Are you still there?' asked a baffled DJ Liz Anya.

'Emh heah, Zee Hay Zithh Agya! Zhankh ooo, zho mush! Vhyy!' Nanny Gigg took the phone out of her mouth and repeated herself. 'Sorry! I'm here, DJ Liz Anya! Thank you so much! Bye!'

'Samantha! Ajay!' she roared, walking around the kitchen on her hands, 'WE'RE GOING TO SEE THE SCOOOOONES!!'

'We'll be there in a minute, Nanny Gigg!' yelled Sam, wrinkling her ginger eyebrows. She didn't usually like being called Samantha – she much preferred to be called Sam – but from the look of the pink slippers bobbing around behind the kitchen window she could see that Nanny Gigg was having a bit of a *moment*, and she decided to let it go.

Sam grabbed the twine holding the tightly packed straw together and pulled, while Ajay got behind and pushed. The huge bale hardly moved. 'C'mon, Ajay, push harder – we've got to change the bedding in the llama enclosure!'

Sam had opened her animal sanctuary in the long back garden of her granny's house only a few months before, but already Hannigan's Haven was home to seventy-two animals – from the everyday dogs, cats, moles, voles and pot-bellied pigs, to the more exotic koala bears, pythons and blue-eyed cockatoos. The Haven even had a tiny pygmy hippo called Gregory.

Nanny Gigg's house was right in the centre of Clobberstown, and the kids in the area called it 'Clobberstown Zoo'. Some of the smaller ones sometimes knocked at the back gate and offered money to come in for a look, but Sam always let them in for free and gave them a guided tour, introducing each animal by name.

Sam loved animals and was delighted when other kids wanted to know more about them, but her favourite was Barker, a huge, furry, slightly orange, friendly old mutt of a dog. Apart from Ajay, and Nanny Gigg of course, Barker was Sam's best pal. Ajay loved Barker too – like Sam, he loved all animals – but he preferred the kind of animals that most people didn't like so much: creepy crawlies, snakes, scorpions and spiders were *his* favourites. He even had a pet tarantula spider called Tadhg.

Sam grunted in frustration. Despite all their pushing and pulling, the hay bale was still stubbornly refusing to budge. Barker bounded over to Sam, snagged the twine between her teeth and tried to help. 'Good girl, Barker,' said Sam through gritted teeth. 'Clever girl!'

'Holy moley,' said Ajay, 'we'll have to order smaller bales of hay next time – this one's too big to shift!'

Just then a massive, hairy hand the size of a dinner plate appeared in the space between Sam and Ajay. It grabbed the hay bale with jumbo sausage-sized fingers and lifted it over both of their heads.

The massive, hairy hand was attached to a massive, hairy arm, which in turn was attached to a massive, hairy man called Ogg. Ogg was the caretaker at St Gobnet's, the local school that Sam and Ajay went to, and he helped out at Hannigan's Haven for an hour after school each day. Although he was over two metres tall with a monobrow and muscles like overstuffed bags of cement, he was as gentle and good-natured as a St Bernard puppy. Sam often wondered what the animal sanctuary would do without him – especially for the heavy lifting.

'Where Ogg put hay?' asked Ogg.

'The ... llamas …' gasped Sam, out of breath.

'K.O.' boomed Ogg. 'Watch out, Gertie and Delilah – incoming!'

With that, the enormous handyman tossed the hay bale over the fence into the enclosure like he was throwing a family pack of popcorn. Gertie and Delilah sidestepped and the hefty bale thudded heavily into the space between them.

'Thanks ... Ogg ...' said Ajay, wiping sweat off his forehead and brushing his jet-black hair out of his eyes.

At the end of the garden, behind the many pens, hutches, coops and corrals, the door of a tumbledown wooden out-house slowly creaked open. A pair of mischievous brown eyes squinted out from under a mop of mischievous-looking brown hair. The eyes belonged to Bruno, Sam's slightly older brother, and they were always on the lookout for monkey business.

Bruno smirked and inspected the small green bottle he held in his hand. *Another successful raid on the inventing shed*, he thought.

Sam and Bruno's granddad, Daddy Mike, had gone missing years ago, leaving behind a very sad Nanny Gigg and a shed full of the most amazing inventions. On shelves and hanging on hooks on the walls were astounding doo-dads, gizmos and whatyoumaycallits that Daddy Mike had invented, such as the Freeze-Ray 2000, the Brain Swap 3000, Stay-Put Putty and the Clone-O-Matic mini-duplicator.

All of them were covered in dirt, dust and cobwebs, and Bruno hadn't much of a clue about what any of them actually did. This lack of understanding however didn't stop him from trying out the various contraptions on his poor sister. Over the years Sam had found herself stuck high up on walls with Stay-Put Putty, had her fingernails and toenails turned bright green by the Fancy-Fingers 200, and been brain-swapped with Barker the dog for almost a week thanks to the Brain Swap 3000. That's why she felt so close to Barker – she had walked a mile in her paws!

Bruno lifted the green bottle up to the sky. The liquid inside looked like it was glowing. The handwritten label on the bottle read, 'ENORMA-GRO 3000. WARNING: USE ONE DROP ONLY – A LITTLE GOES A LONG WAY!'

Hmmmm, thought Bruno, *if a little goes a long way, how long a way will a LOT go?*

Bruno crept up quietly behind Sam and Ajay, who were spreading the hay out for Gertie and Delilah's bedding. He skulked past Kevin the sloth's cage and slithered over to the small hutch where Egbert the hamster lived. Kevin, hanging upside down from his oak branch, opened one sleepy eye to look at Bruno, then drifted off again into a deep, drowsy doze.

Bruno opened up Egbert's hutch and took out a small dish of hamster food pellets. He gave them a sniff. *Ugh*, thought Bruno, *smells gross – but I bet they'll taste lovely with a little drop of ENORMA-GRO 3000!*

He twisted off the top of the bottle and, looking shiftily around to make sure no-one could see what he was up to, carefully dripped one drop of the bright-green liquid over the small brown pellets of food.

There was a sizzling noise. Egbert, who had been playing in a pile of cotton wool balls in the corner of the hutch, scampered over to the door, wondering what the curly-haired human was doing to his food.

Egbert really is quite a small hamster, thought Bruno. Maybe another couple of drops wouldn't hurt?

He tipped two more drops onto Egbert's feed and quickly put the dish back in the hutch and shut the door. Then he stood back and leaned innocently against the side of the koala pen. *Now, let's see what this ENORMA-GRO stuff can do!*

Inside the hutch, Egbert advanced on the food and gave one of the pellets a nibble. *YUM! I don't know what that human put on my grub but it's given it a very moreish flavour!* He tucked in with gusto, licking his lips with his little hamster tongue, and soon the dish was empty and the tiny hamster was full. Egbert let out a small burp.

By the koala pen, Bruno checked his watch, eager for some action. He looked at the bottle label again. *Maybe I should give him another drop?*

Suddenly a shrill, squeaky noise, like the sound of balloons being twisted, came from Egbert's hutch. Bruno's eyes widened – the excruciating noise was getting louder.

'What is that *horrible* noise?' shouted Sam as she and Ajay hurried across from the llama enclosure. Ogg bounded over from where he was feeding Sharon the pelican, his fingers in his ears and his eyes scrunched shut.

'Egbert's cage!' cried Ajay. 'Look – it's getting bigger!'

He was right – Egbert's wooden hutch seemed to be bowing outward at the sides and the roof, as if it was being blown up like a timber blimp. The wooden panels started to splinter and bend, and then they burst open and fell to the ground, revealing a huge, furry, chubby-cheeked monster with two sharp protruding teeth. He sat on cotton balls in the remains of the hutch and looked at the kids with red eyes. Ajay shrieked!

'Egbert,' asked Sam, 'is that you?'

Hearing his name, the massive hamster got up on his paws and hopped over the broken bits of splintered wood that used to be his hutch. As Sam and Ajay looked on in amazement, the once tiny rodent seemed to be getting bigger and bigger – he was now up to Sam's waist, the size of a farmyard pig. Egbert looked around him with bright, panicky red eyes.

'He's scared,' said Ajay, and he held up a piece of lettuce. 'Here boy, heeeere Egbert, I have some tasty lettuce for you.'

Egbert looked at the lettuce for a moment, licked his furry lips, and then ran full tilt at Ajay, his big paws slapping the ground as he went. Ajay dived to one side but the enormous hamster kept going, running head-first into the gate of the sloth's cage – almost, but not quite, waking Kevin up. Stirred by the commotion, birds started screeching and animals began to chatter and howl excitedly. Sharon the pelican *grawwked* loudly and shook out her enormous feathered wings.

Egbert sat on the ground by the koala pen, dazed and blinking. Ogg sat down beside him and stroked his fur. The giant, shivering hamster snuggled gratefully into the hefty handyman.

'What happened to him?' asked Sam. 'Or should I say, WHO happened to him?'

Bruno, who had been standing back, looking innocent and watching the fun, couldn't contain himself any more. He erupted in a torrent of giggles, which soon became a gush of loud guffaws.

'BRUNO!' shouted Sam. 'What did you do to poor Egbert?!'

Bruno's mean-spirited cackling settled down to a quiet but equally mean-spirited snicker. 'I just gave him a drop or two of this

ENORMA-GRO stuff in his food,' he said, holding up the small green bottle with the glowing liquid inside. 'I thought we'd all get a BIG laugh out of it!'

Sam stormed over to Bruno. 'ENORMA-GRO?? Give that here!' she said, snatching the bottle out of his hands. 'You fiend, Bruno! Look what you've done to that poor hamster! I'm going to tell Nanny Gigg to put the padlock back on the inventing shed.'

Ogg looked down at Egbert. He was sure he had seen another bottle in the inventing shed with a label that read SHRINKTASTIC 4000 – could that get the poor not-so-little hamster back to his normal size? 'I think I know how to shrink Egbert,' he said to Sam. 'Leave it to Ogg.'

'Thanks, Ogg,' said Sam, petting the hamster on his enormous furry head. 'Don't worry, Eggie, Ogg always knows what to do.' She gave Bruno a thunderous look and stalked off towards the kitchen door.

After picking up the empty dish of hamster food so the other animals wouldn't lick it and get a touch of the old Egberts, Ajay followed her.

Unnoticed by either Sam or Ajay, Bruno took another small bottle of ENORMA-GRO from his pocket. He looked through the kitchen window at Sindy the budgie and smirked, another devious, dastardly plan already hatching in his mind.

In the kitchen Nanny Gigg was still walking around on her hands. Her feet waggled wildly in the air as she plodded around excitedly. One slipper had fallen off. Sindy the budgie looked down at the mayhem from the top of a kitchen cupboard. Nanny Gigg noticed the kids coming in and, with a mighty bounce from her skinny arms, flipped over deftly onto her feet. Sindy fluttered down and, deciding it was safe again to do so, resumed her usual perch on Nanny Gigg's shoulder.

'Kiddos!' cried Gigg. 'Great news! The Greatest of great news! The bestest, brilliantest, most marvelously mega news ever!'

'The three of us,' she continued, 'are going ... to see ... the Roaming Scones!!'

'The who?' said Ajay.

'No,' cried Nanny Gigg, 'not *The Who*, the Roaming Scones! My favourite rock band from way back when!'

'But Nanny Gigg,' said Sam, 'we have to check on poor Egbert – Bruno made him gro–'

'Stop right there!' said Nanny Gigg. 'I've bigger fish to fry today than Bruno Hannigan!' She smiled wide, took out her false teeth, wiped them on the sleeve of her cardigan and popped them back in again. She looked at Sam and Ajay, and a crinkle appeared amongst all the other wrinkles between her eyes. 'Anyway, I can't believe you have never heard of the Roaming Scones. Pah. Young people nowadays. Come with me.'

Sam wanted to argue but kept her mouth shut. Nanny Gigg looked like she was on a mission, and when Nanny Gigg was on a mission, there was no stopping her!

Nanny Gigg led them upstairs and stopped outside her bedroom door. 'Now then,' she said, 'you know the rules.'

Obediently, Sam and Ajay looked away as Nanny Gigg entered four separate combinations on the four separate locks that kept would-be intruders out of her room. When the last lock, which was opened by entering a series of eighteen secret letters and numbers that only Nanny Gigg knew, popped open, Gigg swung the door wide.

Although Sam was closer to her granny than to any other human being on the face of the Earth, Ajay included, she had never seen the inside of Nanny Gigg's bedroom. She had just assumed that it must be full of hats. Gigg seemed to have a hat for every conceivable occasion – Robin Hood hats for walks in Clobberstown Forest, explorer's pith helmets for shopping expeditions, and lovely cowboy hats for posh dinners – but when they walked into the bedroom, there were no hats on display.

Every millimetre of wall space was taken up with posters of a pair of wrinkly men, one with mirrored glasses and long, dyed-black hair, the other with blue eyes and curly grey hair festooned with beads and ribbons. Their clothes made them look like they had both recently graduated, as (very) mature students, from pirate school.

On each poster the two far-out fellows were striking a different pose: in some they had their hands on their hips, in others they both pouted at the camera with crinkly, wrinkly lips. In a few of them the curly-haired guy cradled a sparkling guitar in his arms, a guitar that seemed to be made of solid gold.

'That's Eddie,' said Nanny Gigg, pointing to the ancient dude with the long black hair, 'and that's my darling Pete.' She blew a kiss at the curly-haired codger with the golden guitar and sighed deeply. Sam and Ajay exchanged a look. They had never seen Nanny Gigg look so ... *fluttery*.

'Me and Daddy Mike used to love them, they were never off our record player,' said Nanny Gigg wistfully.

'Your record *what*?' asked Ajay, but Nanny Gigg wasn't listening.

'The Scones had all the hits,' said Gigg, sighing again. '"The Girl with the Stars in Her Hair", "I Wanna Love You, Girl", "My Little Girl Has Gone Away"...'

'Did they have any songs that weren't about girls?' asked Sam.

'Actually, now I come to think of it, no they didn't,' said Gigg. 'They were mostly about girls, all right. But they were great songs – they all had a great beat that you could really dance to.' Nanny Gigg scrunched up her eyes, gritted her false teeth and waved her arms wildly while grunting out a tune: '*Urgh, urgh, urgh-urgh, doo doo. Urgh, urgh, urgh-urgh, doo doo.*' It didn't sound like any tune that Sam had ever danced to.

'So what do you say?' asked Nanny Gigg. 'Would you like to go and see the Scones with me tomorrow night? Three VIP tickets! I'll ask Ogg to stay over to look after Bruno and the animals.'

'Emmmm,' said Ajay, thinking of a whole night listening to two elderly gentlemen singing songs about girls. It didn't have a huge amount of instant appeal to either of the kids. 'Wouldn't it be better if Bruno went instead of me?' asked Ajay. 'There's only three tickets and I would hate to break up the family.'

Nanny Gigg shook her head firmly. 'No way,' she said. 'Bruno is not allowed anywhere next nor near my Eddie and Pete. He drew moustaches on a picture of them in one of my music magazines.

He can stay here with Ogg and muck out the animals.' Nanny Gigg grinned and waggled her grey eyebrows. 'Did I mention there's a slap-up dinner and a night in a posh bed and breakfast included in the prize …'

Sam and Ajay exchanged a glance. 'SOLD!' they cried together. The prospect of a yummy feast, a comfy bed, as well as a breakfast the next morning that wasn't made by Nanny Gigg, sounded great. Nanny Gigg loved to cook but had fairly strange ideas about what foods actually went together. Sam was no stranger to cornflakes covered in melted cheese, or pancakes spread with guacamole, so breakfast made by someone else – someone who made yummy breakfasts for a living! – sounded to Sam like a holiday for her taste buds.

'And, best of all,' said Nanny Gigg, looking more excited than ever, 'we get to meet Eddie and Pete before the show!!'

'Yay …' said Sam and Ajay in unison.

Nanny Gigg jumped up on her bed, her arms outstretched. Sindy fluttered off Gigg's shoulder, looking a bit fed up with another disruption. 'WE'RE GOING TO SEE THE ROAMING SCOOOOOOONNNNNNESSS!!'

CHAPTER TWO
ABSOLUTELY CRACKERS

Nanny Gigg was so over-excited by the idea of seeing her beloved Eddie and Pete that she had to have a lie down. She ordered Sam and Ajay out of her room and they went down the rickety stairs to the kitchen, with Sindy perched on Sam's finger.

Ajay went out to check on Egbert the hamster while Sam put on the kettle. Sam had known Ajay for what seemed like forever – they had met on their very first day in St Gobnet's National School. Sam, who was quite small for her age, arrived at the school in the passenger seat of Big Bertha, Nanny Gigg's enormous amphibious vehicle. Kind of like a motor boat mixed with a monster truck, Big Bertha was equally at home in water or on the road, and Nanny Gigg really only used it for big occasions like birthdays, holidays or, in this case, Sam's first day at school.

The first person Sam spoke to that day was a little boy with black hair and a magnifying glass the size of a basketball hoop. He was down on his hands and knees in the yard, staring at something on the ground. 'What are you looking at? Are you a defective?' asked Sam.

'A *detective*?' said the little boy. 'No, I just love animals. Especially creepy-crawlies like this – have a look!'

Sam got down on her knees and peered through the magnifying glass at a line of ants carrying what looked like half a packet of crisps across the tarmac.

'Ants can carry fifty times their own body weight,' said Ajay, looking over Sam's shoulder. 'I love ants. I love spiders. I love insects. I have a caterpillar called Twitchy who lives in my shed. One day he's going to turn into a flutterby.'

'You mean a *butterfly*?' said Sam.

'Do you want to come to my house after school and meet Twitchy?' asked Ajay.

'Yes, please. I love animals too,' said Sam. And that was it, friends forever.

Ajay came back in from the yard. 'Egbert's fine, he's nearly back to normal size,' he said. 'Ogg found some sort of shrinking antidote-thingy in the shed that seemed to work a treat.'

Sam smiled from ear to ear. 'Clever Ogg. I knew he'd think of something! Okay,' she said, as they sat down at the kitchen table with mugs of hot tea, 'it's Friday tomorrow, so that means it's Show & Tell. What have we got to show this week?'

Sam and Ajay were famous in St Gobnet's for bringing in strange and unusual animal-related odds and ends for their highly strung teacher Ms Sniffles's Friday Show & Tell session. The previous Friday they brought in a snakeskin shed by Marvin, one of the corn snakes that lived in Hannigan's Haven. That made Ms Sniffles jump, but it was nothing compared to the week before when Ajay brought in his pet tarantula spider, Tadgh. Ms Sniffles was so discombobulated she locked herself in the staff room and, much to the annoyance of the other teachers, ate all the biscuits.

Hmmm, thought Ajay, *what could we bring in?* He looked at Sindy the budgie, who, being petrified of the kettle, had fluttered off Sam's finger while she was making tea, and was now perched on Ajay's finger instead. 'What about Sindy?' he said.

'No, Annie Corcoran brought in a budgie last month,' said Sam.

'But her budgie didn't talk,' said Ajay.

'Neither does Sindy,' countered Sam.

'Aha! Not yet!' smiled Ajay. He looked at his watch. 'We've both done our homework and the next feeding time is six o'clock. That means we have almost an hour and a half to teach Sindy to speak!'

They spent the next hour and a half trying to get the little blue-feathered budgie to say *Sindy wants a cracker*, but the best they could get out of the obstinate avian was a few half-hearted squawks, none of which sounded anything like *Sindy* or *cracker*. 'Maybe we could teach her to ride a little budgie-sized bike?' suggested Ajay.

'Two problems with that,' said Sam. 'Firstly, we don't have a little budgie-sized bike, and secondly' – she pointed up at the kitchen wall clock – 'it's feeding time. We'll just have to bring Sindy into school as she is.'

Sam put Sindy into the birdcage on the counter and the small budgie hopped onto her swing. 'Crackers!' she squawked.

'She did it! Good old Sindy!' cried Ajay, and smiling with relief, they both went out to feed the animals.

As they left the kitchen, the door from the TV room creaked open and Bruno stuck his curly head round. He looked at Sindy, swinging happily in her cage, and his lips lifted into a roguish smile. *Hee hee,* he thought, *I bet I can teach that bird to speak …* He picked up the birdcage by the handle at the top and quietly brought Sindy upstairs to his bedroom.

The next morning Sam came down to the kitchen, where Nanny Gigg was making breakfast, shuffling around the kitchen and waggling her bum to a Roaming Scones song that was on the radio. 'Ahhhh, Sammy-baby,' she cried when she noticed her granddaughter come in, 'this is a smashing tune – "Boogie Girl Boogie" – one of the Scones' greats!'

The song ended and Nanny Gigg clapped her hands excitedly. 'Waffles this morning,' she said brightly as Sam sat down at the table.

Waffles? thought Sam. *Yum!*

'Waffles with brown sauce,' said Gigg, 'just the way you like them.' She put down the plate in front of Sam, who sniffed at the waffles and tried to scrape off some of the brown sauce with a knife. Sam dropped a waffle down to Barker, who was in her usual place under the kitchen table. Barker ate it greedily. She liked brown sauce, even if it *was* slightly inappropriate on breakfast food.

'Nanny Gigg,' said Sam, slipping her second waffle under the table to Barker, 'do you mind if I bring Sindy into school today for Show & Tell?'

Nanny Gigg beamed. 'I'm sure she'd love that, Sam. She loves kids. It's just teachers she has a problem with!'

Sam grabbed her schoolbag and plucked the birdcage off the counter.

'Oh!' added Nanny Gigg. 'Don't forget we're going to see the Roaming Scones tonight! I'll pick you up in Big Bertha after school!' She punched the air, nearly dislodging her false teeth. 'THE ROAMING SCOOOOONES!!!'

Sam scrunched up her face in embarrassment and Sindy let out a happy-sounding squawk as they trotted down the garden path. Well, Sam trotted. Sindy just sat there in her cage, swinging on her swing.

Ajay's house was halfway between Hannigan's Haven and St Gobnet's, and, as usual, he was waiting for Sam at his garden gate. 'Did you have any luck getting Sindy to talk last night?' asked Ajay, peering into the cage.

'No,' said Sam. 'When I came in from feeding the animals Sindy wasn't in the kitchen. I think Nanny Gigg might have taken her upstairs to show her those funny posters of Petey and Ed.'

'Eddie and Pete,' said Ajay.

'That's what I said!' laughed Sam, walking through the school gate and running over to Ogg, who was wearing blue overalls and polishing the school sign in his role as caretaker at St Gobnet's. Egbert the hamster, now returned to his normal size, was peeping out of the chest pocket of Ogg's overalls.

'Found SHRINKTASTIC stuff in inventing shed. Worked a treat!' boomed Ogg as Egbert chirruped happily.

Just after little break, Ms Sniffles kicked off Show & Tell. It was a tradition that children would bring in objects from their home every

Friday to show the class and talk about. These objects could be weird and wonderful, such as the giant sculpture of President Michael D. Higgins made from recycled plastic milk cartons that Jack Byrne had brought in (it had taken his brother Alfie three weeks to make, and he had to drink thirty-two litres of milk to get all the cartons); or they could be fairly ordinary but much loved, like the threadbare, one-eyed, one-legged cuddly puppy called Scamp that Grace Whelan had shown to everyone the previous week. Sam and Ajay usually worked as a team and brought in something from Hannigan's Haven or from Ajay's large collection of spiders, snakes and assorted pet insects.

This week Abbie Cuffe had brought in her uncle's artificial leg to show. She said he was asleep when she took it and she'd have to get it back to him straight after school as he was meeting his girlfriend at four o'clock. Ms Sniffles looked at her watch. 'Don't worry, Abbie, you'll make it in plenty of time.' She took a deep breath through her teeth. 'All right Sam and Ajay, let's see what you've brought in.'

Sam brought the birdcage up to the top of the class. She had covered it up with her coat during class to muffle the sound of Sindy's squawks, and now she took it off with a flourish. 'Ta-daa!' she cried. 'Ladles and jellyspoons, I mean, ladies and gentlemen, boys and girls, I give you ... Sindy, the amazing talking budgie!'

Sam pointed at Sindy to give her the cue to perform, but the little blue budgie stayed quiet. 'The amazing Sindy, the chit-chatting wonder of Clobberstown!' cried Sam. Sindy didn't even as much as squeak.

Ajay took an iced ring biscuit out of his lunchbox and waved it at the cage. 'C'mon Sindy,' he whispered. 'Say *Sindy wants a cracker* like a good little birdy.'

Sam looked down at the class. All the kids were staring up at the silent Sindy. Some were resting their chins on their hands – they were starting to get bored. She put her nose up to the bars of the birdcage. 'Good budgie, Sindy, say *Sindy wants a cracker* and I'll give you some nice birdseed!'

Sindy looked up at Sam, pecked her on the nose and squawked, 'Sindy wants ... KNICKERS!' Ms Sniffles fell off her teacher's chair in shock.

'KNICKERS!' squawked the small blue budgie,

'KNICKERS!!

'KNICKERS!!!'

Sam quickly threw her coat over the birdcage, and Sindy fell silent once more. She looked down at her classmates, who stared back goggle-eyed, each mouth a perfect O shape. Suddenly the whole class erupted in raucous laughter, screeching nearly as loudly as Sindy had done moments before. A delighted-looking Abbie Cuffe was waving a homework copy over Ms Sniffles's face in an effort to revive her.

The bell went for big break and Sam grabbed the birdcage. Ajay held the door open and they quickly scurried out into the yard. The sound of their classmates' laughter still rumbled through the prefab classroom windows. Sam lifted her coat up and peered into the birdcage. Sindy looked like she was smiling. 'I bet my ratbag big brother Bruno is behind this ...' she growled to Ajay, rubbing her nose where Sindy had pecked her.

After school they waited at the gates for Nanny Gigg to arrive and pretty soon, the thundering sound of Big Bertha's engine could be heard as the big monster-boat-truck trundled up the road.

Nanny Gigg stopped outside the school and saluted the lollipop lady. 'Hi Sheila! We're off to see the Scones tonight!'

'Lucky ducks!' replied Sheila, who must have been a similar age to Gigg.

Sam was climbing aboard when she realised she was still holding Sindy's birdcage. 'Nanny Gigg,' she shouted over the roar of the engine, 'we'll have to drop Sindy home!'

Nanny Gigg pulled on her leather fighter pilot's helmet (she really did have a hat for every occasion) and flipped down its goggles. 'No time!' she shouted back. 'We'll be late for the Scones! We will have to bring her! Come on, Ajay, climb aboard and buckle up! I have an overnight bag packed for each of you, and a Jolly Roger™ Chew Bar for the journey!'

When they were all safely onboard with their seatbelts on, Sam took the Jolly Roger™ Chew Bar out of its bright-blue wrapper and bit into it. *Yum, fruit-flavoured, chewy goodness.*

Ajay took the birdcage to hold on his knee. 'Sam,' he whispered, 'I hope they don't have a no-pets policy at this B&B ...'

32

My Tube

AjayPatel3

✔ 107 SUBSCRIBERS

HOME
VIDEOS · PLAYLISTS · 🔍

33

THAT'S THE, UM, BREAKFAST PART.

BUT BEFORE WE GO TO BED, WE'RE GOING TO SEE THE SCONES!!

WOOOOO-HOOOOOOOO!!! IT'S THE SHOWJUMP ARENA, RIGHT THERE!

YAY. THE ROAMING SCONES AT THE SHOWJUMP ARENA. NEARLY FORGOT.

I JUST HOPE THEY ALLOW BIRDS INTO THE B'N'B.

WE'RE HERE!

OH MY DOG!

WOOOOOOOWWWWW... DON'T FORGET TO LIKE AND SUBSCRIBE!

CHAPTER THREE
GIGG OF THE CENTURY

'Holy moley,' said Nanny Gigg, pulling in to the gravel driveway. She wrenched up the handbrake and Big Bertha screeched to a halt, raising up a cloud of dust and peppering the front door with a barrage of small stones.

The house was beautiful, covered in luscious green ivy so thick that it almost obscured the eight big windows at the front. A fancy Roman column stood at either side of the massive red wooden door, which, to Sam's surprise, swung open violently.

'What is the meaning of this?!' piped a high-pitched, squeaky voice from the doorway. A tall, skinny man emerged. He had a mop of untidy wiry grey hair on his head and gigantic coarse, bristly grey sideburns at either side of his thin face. At the end of his long nose he wore a tiny pair of spectacles that seemed to only stay in place by pinching the tip of his snout.

'It's our guests, Percival,' boomed a deeper voice from behind him. 'Don't you remember?'

The bony man adjusted his yellow bowtie and brushed down the lapels of his brown tweed jacket as he was joined by a sizeable woman, also dressed head to toe in chequered tweed. 'Hello, guests!' she bellowed over the sound of Big Bertha's engine. A toothy but not entirely convincing smile filled her face.

Nanny Gigg switched off the engine. 'Hello, yourself,' she said, nimbly hopping down from the driver's seat. 'We have a booking, Hannigan for three?'

'The Roaming Scones contest winners, yes of course,' said the deep-voiced woman, still speaking very loudly even though the only sound from Big Bertha was a gentle ticking as the engine cooled. 'You're not our, ahem, *usual* sort of guest, I must say. Still, beggars can't be choosers. You are our *only* guests this weekend, as it happens.' She sniffed noisily, her nose wrinkled as if she was smelling something she didn't much like. 'I am Margaret-Elizabeth Snoot, the owner of the Duck & Duvet Exclusive Bed & Breakfast Posh-Home-Away-From-Posh-Home, and this is my husband, Percival.' She clicked her fingers. 'Percival! Get their bags, would you?'

'Yes, Margaret-Elizabeth,' said Percival as he scuttled over to the side of the big boat-truck. Sam and Ajay started to hand down their backpacks and Sindy's birdcage. At the sight of the small budgie, Percival's mouth arranged itself in a grimace of alarm, revealing a disconcerting selection of yellow, stumpy teeth. 'Margaret-Elizabeth,' he shrilled, 'it's a ... a ... b-b-b-bird!'

'Ah,' rumbled Margaret-Elizabeth, 'I had feared this when I discovered that children were coming. Children are notorious for liking ... *ugh* ... animals. We don't allow guests to bring animals into our bed and breakfast' – she glared at the birdcage – 'especially animals of the *avian* variety.'

Nanny Gigg scratched her head.

'She means birds, Nanny,' said Sam.

'Yes!' bellowed Margaret-Elizabeth. 'I mean, no! No birds allowed. Hate the little blighters. You'll have to leave it in your, ahem, car.'

Sam looked outraged. 'But it'll be cold out here – poor Sindy will freeze! Anyway, your bed & breakfast is called DUCK & Duvet, you should *welcome* birds!'

Margaret-Elizabeth furrowed her considerable eyebrows and stuck out her lower lip. 'NO birds,' she said firmly, 'Duck & Duvet policy.'

Ajay looked in at Sindy, all alone in the cage. 'Don't worry, Sindy,' he whispered, 'I've got a plan.' He quickly took the Jolly Roger™ Chew Bar with its bright-blue wrapper from his jacket pocket, opened the birdcage door and put his hand inside. He swapped the Chew Bar for the budgie and gently bundled Sindy into his inside pocket. 'Ssssshhhhh,' he said to the little bird, 'that Chew Bar is about the same size and colour as you. I can smuggle you into the B&B and that posh pair will never know… as long as you keep the noise down and they don't look too closely at the cage!'

'Welcome to the Duck & Duvet, I suppose,' said Margaret-Elizabeth sullenly as she led them through the red door and into the hallway. A large wooden keyholder hung on the wall beside painted landscapes and pictures of showjumping horses.

Percival Snoot reached out his bony, tweed-clad arm and whipped down a silver key with #11 on its black plastic keyring. He thrust it at Nanny Gigg, who took the key and bit it between her false teeth like a pirate testing the authenticity of a gold doubloon. 'Top of the stairs, first room on the right,' said Percival, a look of distaste clouding his ferret-like features.

'Breakfast is served between seven-fifteen and eight-forty-five,' said Margaret-Elizabeth. 'One minute earlier or one moment later than that and you and your party will not gain admission to the breakfast room.' She gestured to a door through which could be seen five smallish tables, each one made up for breakfast with knives and forks, napkins and teacups.

Sam's eyes widened. In the corner of the breakfast room was an old, beaten-up-looking wicker basket and inside, resting on a worn-out tartan blanket, was the biggest (and maybe the oldest) St Bernard dog Sam had ever seen. He was chubby with thick brown and white fur, and he snored gently as he slept. 'What a GORGEOUS doggo!' cried Sam as she rushed over to the basket.

The dog opened a sleepy eye, stuck out a lolling tongue and meekly wagged his tail. Sam couldn't help herself – she knew the people who ran the place were a bit snobbish, but she just had to – and she hugged the enormous dog. 'Hello, fella,' she said happily, her face half buried in soft brown fur.

'Get away from that mutt,' boomed Margaret-Elizabeth. 'You'll catch fleas and I don't want to have to pay for you to be deloused.'

'But he's so lovely and cuddly and tubby and loveable,' protested Sam, who was soon joined by Ajay, both hugging and petting the dog, who was now quite awake and wagging his tail with abandon.

'Tubbs is not sanitary,' piped up Percival in his high, flute-like voice. 'Leave it alone, will you? We can't get rid of it – it belonged to my dear departed mother.'

On hearing Percival mention his previous owner, Tubbs let out a small, doggy whine.

'Shut your noise, mutt,' growled Percival menacingly. (Well, as menacingly as his high-pitched voice would allow.)

'Oh,' said Nanny Gigg. 'I'm so sorry to hear that about your poor mother.'

'No, no,' interrupted Margaret-Elizabeth, 'she's not kicked the bucket, we've had her put in a home. Now if you will *please* retire to your room.' She pointed upstairs with a meaty finger.

'C'mon, kids,' said Nanny Gigg brightly. 'We have to get ready for the Scones anyway, time to say goodnight to Tubbs.'

With some regret, Sam and Ajay tore themselves away from the colossal cuddly canine and stomped up the stairs after Nanny Gigg. Sam had the feeling that the Snoots didn't care very much for that woman's poor ex-dog. *Maybe I'll pop down later*, she thought, *and give him a treat*. She always carried a few Jolly Roger™ Dog Biscuits around with her in case of emergencies like this.

They trooped up the deluxe wooden staircase, and, once inside their room, they each chose one of the three single beds. Nanny Gigg locked the door. 'We don't want that plummy pair of Snoots barging in, do we?' she said. 'Right, I'm off to get changed for the show!'

'Hold on, Nanny,' said Sam, 'what about the slap-up dinner we were promised?'

Ajay stopped unpacking his backpack and looked over. He was quite hungry.

'Ooooohhhh, yesssss …' said Nanny Gigg. 'One slap-up dinner, coming up!' She opened the top flap of her own backpack and took out a picnic basket. She whipped the duvet off her bed, set it down on the floor and started laying out the contents of the picnic basket on top. 'It's more a slap-up *picnic* than a slap-up *dinner* – this way we don't have to wait in a restaurant so we'll have more time for Eddie and Pete!'

The picnic basket was full of food, some of it reasonably normal like cheese sandwiches and cartons of juice, and some of it weird and wonderful 'Nanny Gigg specials' like ham and custard rolls. Sam was a vegetarian so she wouldn't have eaten these anyway but Ajay, who was used to Nanny Gigg's curious culinary creations, tucked into the rolls hungrily, licking his lips with delight.

After they ate, Nanny Gigg took her bag and went into the bathroom to change. 'Those snooty Snoots don't seem to like their dog very much, do they?' said Ajay.

'Poor Tubbs, he has a dog's life here,' agreed Sam. 'That Percival fella is for the birds.'

'Birds!' cried Ajay. 'Holy moley, I forgot about Sindy!' He grabbed his jacket off the bed and reached into the inside pocket. Sindy started to cheep. 'Sssssshhhh, Sindy, the Snoots will hear you,' he said. 'Poor thing, she'll be starv– Hold on, I can't get her out! She's stuck!'

Sam came over to the side of the bed.

'I don't understand it,' said Ajay. 'She went in easy enough, but now she's too big to get back out! Maybe she ate all the birdseed I was keeping in my pocket and she's stuck because she's too full?'

He gave a massive tug and the budgie popped out. Ajay sat down on the carpet, holding the blue-feathered bird in his lap.

'Oh my dog!' exclaimed Sam. 'The *size* of her! She's as big as a parrot!'

Ajay gaped at the not-so-small budgie. 'You're right! She's definitely grown! But *how?*'

'I'll tell you how,' said Sam. 'One word: Bruno Hannigan!'

'That's two words, but I bet you're right. He must have put some of that ENORMA-GRO stuff into Sindy's birdseed and Sindy ate it when she was in my pocket. That's *so* Bruno – that must be why she's growing!' Ajay frowned. A very unpleasant thought had just occurred to him. 'Sam, we don't know how much ENORMA-GRO Bruno gave to Sindy. And the bigger the dose …'

'… the bigger the bird!' cried Sam. Suddenly there was a sound like balloons being twisted. In Ajay's lap, Sindy gave a small *squawk* and, with a FRRROPPPPPP-ing sound, her body instantly expanded by five centimetres all round. Sindy was now the size of a large seagull.

Just then Nanny Gigg appeared in the bathroom doorway. 'Well, kids,' she said, 'whaddya think?'

The ballooning budgie momentarily forgotten, Sam and Ajay gaped at the rock'n'roll vision before them. Instead of her usual pink cardigan, pleated skirt, droopy tights and fluffy slippers, Nanny Gigg was wearing high-heeled red leather pixie boots, a long tee-shirt, fishnet stockings and a battered black leather jacket. She turned around, giving them a twirl and revealing THE ROAMING SCONES written on the back of her jacket in metal studs. She took off her star-shaped sunglasses, adjusted her false teeth and gave them a wink. 'Tell me, am I gorgeous or am I gorgeous?'

Neither of the kids had ever seen Sam's grandmother look quite so strange. Yes, they were used to the different hats, and yes, they were used to the unusual multi-coloured coats and jackets that Nanny Gigg made out of old curtains and bedspreads, but this weird rocker look was a new one on them – Nanny Gigg actually looked like she could be *in* the band. 'You *are* gorgeous!' shouted Sam. 'You look coooooooool, just like a rock star!'

'A rock star granny! Ah, thanks pet!' said Nanny Gigg. 'Now, if we're all fed and watered, let's go to meet the' – she took out three gold-stamped VIP tickets from the zipped pocket on the arm of her leather jacket and started to tremble – 'the …'

'The Roaming Scones?' said Ajay helpfully.

'Yes, Eddie and Pete,' gulped Nanny Gigg. 'We're really going to meet Eddie and Pete … THE Roaming Scones …'

Sam looked down at Sindy. In the short time they were admiring Nanny Gigg, the budgie seemed to have gotten even bigger. 'Emmm, Nanny Gigg,' she said, looking up at her leather-clad grandmother, 'why don't you go on ahead? Ajay and me still have to make ourselves beautiful. You don't want to miss meeting the, ahem, boys. We'll follow you over to the Showjump Arena in a few minutes.'

Nanny Gigg's whole body seemed to be vibrating with excitement. 'Okay,' she said, her voice shaking. 'Okay, good, idea, right on, far out. I'll … I'll just go and meet … Eddie and Pete. The ROAMING SCONES!!!'

With that she scrabbled for the bedroom door handle with her wrinkly hand, unlocked the door and tottered down the stairs on her high-heeled boots. 'See yiz over there!' The front door slammed loudly and she was gone.

CHAPTER FOUR
BIG BIRD

Sam closed the bedroom door and looked at Sindy again. She was definitely growing – she was getting so big Ajay could hardly hold her. He put the bird on the bed and Sindy strutted up and down the duvet on her clawed feet.

'She's the size of a blinkin' Labrador,' said Ajay, 'or a golden retriever. What are we going to do? We can't go to the show and leave her here; the Snoots will hear her squawking, or worse, shouting "KNICKERS" like she did in school. We'll be thrown out of the B&B!'

'Ssshhh, Ajay, can you hear something?' Sam stood with her ear to the bedroom door. Now Nanny Gigg was gone and the house was quiet, a strange noise was echoing up the stairs, bouncing off the carved wooden banisters and reverberating off the high ceiling – a scritching, scratching sound, like someone or something trying to escape from somewhere, digging and gouging with a hard tool or strong claws.

'Tubbs!' cried Sam softly. 'It's Tubbs, I know it is!' Her brow furrowed and she looked at Ajay, her face like thunder. 'Those Snoots must have tied him up or locked him into the breakfast room. That poor dog, he's so big, he's probably bursting for a wee! I'm going down to let him out into the garden.' She opened the door softly and peeped out. *Nobody there*. She turned to Ajay, who was wrestling the huge budgie off the bed – he was afraid Sindy's now-massive claws would tear the bedsheets. 'Back in a mo, don't let Sindy out of the room,' whispered Sam, and she silently padded down the stairs.

Ajay closed the bedroom door and locked it as the balloon-twisting sound echoed through the room. Oh no, he thought, staring goggle-eyed at the gargantuan blue budgerigar standing a metre and a half tall and pecking at the curtains. *Sindy's as big as a pony!*

'Holy moley, Sindy,' said Ajay, 'how much ENORMA-GRO did Bruno put in your feed? Sam is going to marma-lise him!' He looked at his watch – he had to do something. The VIP meet and greet with the Scones in the Showjump Arena was starting any minute – they could forget about making that, but worse, the show itself was starting in the next forty-five minutes. Sam and he couldn't leave Sindy behind in the room like this – she'd peck the place to pieces! Ajay's face brightened as he had an idea. Ogg had used that SHRINKTASTIC stuff to shrink Egbert down to his normal size. Would it work the same way on Sindy? Ajay was sure it would!

He reached past Sindy's enormous pecking beak, grabbed his jacket off the end of his bed and took out his mobile phone. Sindy squawked and gave him a couple of friendly pecks on the shoulder. 'Get off, Sindy,' complained Ajay. 'My phone is powered off, I can't see what I'm doing here.'

Ajay sidled past the immense but amiable budgie and threw open the curtains – to reveal an open window! Sindy gave a louder squawk and ruffled her blue feathers. To Ajay's horror she opened her wings wide and flapped them powerfully, noisily knocking ornaments and photograph frames off the fussy dressing table and the mahogany chest of drawers. With a bound Sindy was in the air and a second later was out the window. *Yikes!*

Ajay quickly stuck his head out. Sindy was in the Duck & Duvet's front garden, perched on a statue in the centre of a water feature and splashing around as if the small fountain was an enormous bird bath. The statue was leaning precariously over to one side under her weight. *Oooh crackers*, Ajay thought, *I think Sam might marma-lise me as well!* He darted out the door and dashed down the ornate staircase, taking it two steps at a time.

Meanwhile, Sam was concentrating so hard on being quiet that she didn't notice the distant commotion. She silently opened the door to the breakfast room and sneaked a look inside. Nobody was there, not even Tubbs, whose untidy basket lay empty in the corner. She could still hear the strange scritching-scratching sound, so she slipped quietly into the room. She looked under the tables, moving each crisp, white tablecloth in turn. 'Tubbs,' she whispered, 'is that you? Where are you?'

Sam stood up quickly as she heard Ajay's noisy descent and the clitch-clatch of the front door opening and closing. 'Ajay?' she whispered. She wondered what he was up to – maybe he had left something in Big Bertha? The scritching-scratching had stopped abruptly with the noise on the stairs, but it started up again now. It seemed to be coming from a door that had the stern words KITCHEN – NO ADMITTANCE written on it in pleasant, flowery letters. Sam raised one eyebrow and went through.

Tubbs was sitting in the middle of the kitchen tiles beside a wide, jagged hole in the floor. He wagged his tail when he saw Sam. The top of a wooden ladder could be seen poking over the edge of the hole. Sam walked quietly over to Tubbs and petted him. 'Hey, boy,' she murmured, 'what's going on here?'

Tubbs grunted a happy doggy grunt and snuggled her as she peered into the darkness of the hole. The scritching-scratching noise has stopped again, and Sam thought she could hear voices coming from the gloom. She strained her ears.

'You imbecile, Percival, don't use the drill! We've almost tunnelled all the way through to the Arena, we don't want to alert the security guards,' said a deep voice that, although far away, sounded to Sam very much like that of Margaret-Elizabeth Snoot.

'Yes, dear,' came the high-pitched reply.

That sounds like Percival! thought Sam. *Tunnelling through to the Showjump Arena? What in the blinkin' barnacles are they up to?*

CHAPTER FIVE
THE TUNESOME TWOSOME

Nanny Gigg was having the best day of her life.

She had walked the short distance from the Duck & Duvet to the Showjump Arena, looking dazzling in her studded leather jacket and tottering precariously in her high-heeled pixie boots. Passersby gaped as she wobbled along unsteadily,  and she gave each a little tinkly wave as she mouthed, 'I'm off to meet the Roaming Scones.'

Arriving at the door of the venue, she was greeted by a smiling security guard who checked her VIP ticket and, once through, a green-uniformed hostess offered Gigg a drink from a silver guitar-shaped tray. 'A nice aperitif?' asked the lady, beaming broadly.

'Oh, *thank* you, my dear,' said Nanny Gigg, smiling back and adjusting her dentures, 'and they're all my own.'

The hostess looked confused for a second. 'Oh! No, madam,' she laughed, 'not "a nice pair of teeth", I meant would you like a *nice aperitif?* A glass of champagne?'

Nanny Gigg cackled. 'Ahh. No thank you, chicken,' she said. 'No champers for me, thanks – I've brought a flask of tea.' She whipped out a tartan-patterned flask from her handbag and unscrewed the top. 'Fancy a cuppa?' She poured herself a cup and followed the bewildered hostess down a long corridor.

'This is the VIP green room,' said the lady, leading Nanny Gigg into a large, high-ceilinged room. 'If you'd like to join the other contest winners, Eddie and Pete from the Roaming Scones will be coming down to meet you shortly.'

Nanny Gigg nearly dropped her flask. She was really going to meet the legendary Eddie and Pete! She walked over to a long table where a group of people were helping themselves to sandwiches, sausage rolls and shrimp in cocktail sauce. Gigg couldn't help noticing that almost everyone at the table had a head of grey or white hair. The ones who had hair, that was. Several of the men piling their plates high with delicious food from the table had no hair at all, and their bald heads glinted and gleamed beneath the large sparkling mirrorball hanging from the ceiling. Everyone had on a Roaming Scones tee-shirt, and most of them were wearing leather jackets, bandanas and biker boots.

One wide, jolly-looking man with a grey moustache shuddered with laughter as he told the story of how he had met the Scones when he was a young boy. 'My mate Jemmy and I didn't have tickets for their gig – we couldn't afford them on our pocket money – so we snuck in the back way without paying. We could see a window up above that was slightly open, so Jemmy got down on his hands and knees and I stood up on his back. I was just about to pull at the frame when the window flew open – and there I was, face to face with Pete Pilchard himself!'

A gasp rose from the group. A couple of granddads mopped their brows. The man continued, 'He just looked at me and says, "Hullo there, who are you?" I told him I was a window cleaner. He gave me some coins and a sandwich off the table behind him and told me to keep up the good work. Then he closed the window – but not before I saw Emmaline leaning up against the table.'

'You saw Emmaline?' said Nanny Gigg, her voice shaking. 'Pete's solid gold guitar?'

The wide man winked at Gigg. 'I was almost close enough to touch her.' He looked around at the group, who were hanging on his every word. 'And that was it. But at least I got to meet Pete – poor Jemmy only got stood on. Of course, I was much smaller then.' They all laughed uproariously at that.

As the laughter died down, there was a little cough from the hostess at the door. 'Ladies and gentlemen, Clobberstown FM contest winners,' she said, 'let me introduce you all to … Eddie Floyd and Pete Pilchard, the Roaming Scones!'

Eddie and Pete bounded into the room, their bangles, bracelets, earrings, necklaces and chains jangling loudly. Pete took off his sunglasses and waved, while Eddie's jet-black hair shone under the mirrorball light. A strange noise started to emerge from the group of elderly fans gathered by the table, a low oooOOOOOOOOOOOHHHHHHHHHHH sound that got louder and louder.

'Guys, guys,' said Pete in his crackling, drawling voice, 'how are ya all doin'?'

On hearing Pete speak, two of the women in the group crumpled to the ground in a faint. A couple of paramedics bustled into the room from the doorway behind the tunesome twosome, checked the ladies' pulses and brought them out on stretchers.

'It's great to be here today,' said Eddie.

'In fact, guys and dolls,' said Pete, 'at our age, it's great to be anywhere.'

The remaining group of contest winners laughed like lunatics at this.

'And it's so lovely to meet you all,' said Eddie. 'Who knew our fans were so young and pretty?'

Another lady swooned and hit the deck. The excitement of meeting the two Scones legends had them dropping like flies.

Eddie stepped over towards Nanny Gigg. 'What's your name, buttercup?' he said, taking her wrinkly hand and kissing it.

'Eeeeeeeeeeeeeeeee, hee hee, heee heeeee,' said Nanny Gigg. 'My name's not Buttercup, Eddie, it's Nanny Gigg!'

'Nanny Gigg,' murmured Eddie softly, 'what a beautiful name. Can I call you Nanny?'

'You can call me anything you want,' said Gigg, 'but just don't call me on Tuesday mornings before eleven, I'll be at yoga.'

'Ah, yoga,' said Pete. 'Eddie and I were into yoga in a big way around the time our red-hot track "I Miss You, Girl" came out, remember?'

'How could I forget, Pete?' said Eddie. 'It went straight to number one, and we were booked to appear on the *Top Hits* TV show.'

'But we couldn't do it, could we, because we were studying yoga with our guru in Tibet, and Eddie here only gets himself tied in a knot trying to do the Elastic Lotus position!'

'Literally tied in a knot,' drawled Eddie, 'my arm over here, my leg under there, my ear under my nose. I was stuck like that for three days. They had to helicopter out a team of Rubik's Cube experts to untie me.'

Pete cackled happily at the memory of this, and Eddie gave him a friendly pat on the back. 'Oh, yes,' he said to the group, 'I nearly forgot. Pete and I have someone we'd like you to meet …'

Just then the doors at the other end of the green room swung open and three burly security men wheeled in a big yellow box that looked very much like it came from an Egyptian pharaoh's tomb, with strange

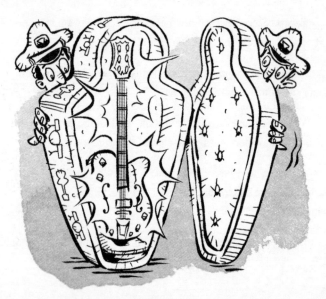

hieroglyphs of musical instruments – guitars, drum kits, pianos, saxophones – painted down the sides. A hush descended on the room. One of the security guards walked reverently around to the front of the wooden box, and, with a theatrical flourish, removed the lid. There was a gasp of awed admiration from the group of fans as Emmaline, Pete Pilchard's fabled solid gold guitar, was revealed in all its jewel-encrusted glory. Nanny Gigg couldn't take her eyes off it. It was so beautiful, maybe even more beautiful than Eddie and Pete. Several of the male contest winners started to cry.

'Twenty kilos of solid gold rock'n'roll goodness,' said Eddie. 'Built over thirty years ago by Egyptian goldsmiths, working under Pete's direction, and encrusted with over two hundred sapphires, emeralds and diamonds from the four corners of the globe. Emmaline has solid silver pickups and platinum volume controls. She even has gold-plated strings, doesn't she, Pete?'

Pete took a soft cloth out of his pocket and started polishing the guitar's shiny golden fretboard. 'Yeaaaaaaahhhhhh, baby,' he said to Emmaline. 'Don't you worry, Emmaline, we'll be onstage rockin' out pretty soon.' He puckered his wrinkly lips and gave the guitar a little kiss.

61

CHAPTER SIX
HEIGH HO, HEIGH HO, IT'S OFF TO ROB WE GO

Sam lay down on the kitchen floor beside Tubbs, her ear close to the opening of the huge tunnel. She listened hard to the voices that were drifting up out of the darkness.

Behind Sam, unnoticed by herself or the massive St Bernard, a wall-mounted TV was showing an Australian soap opera with the sound turned down. The soap was suddenly interrupted by breaking news about a colossal blue parakeet or budgerigar that was terrorising the city. The reporter looked quite frantic as she read out which roads had been blocked and issued dire warnings for people to keep away from the city centre, all the time looking over her shoulder in fear at the giant bird that was perched on top of the General Post Office in O'Connell Street, pecking at the statues.

BREAKING NEWS: GIANT BUDGIE TERRORISES DUBLIN

Tubbs whimpered and put his huge paw on Sam's hand. 'Hush, doggo,' said Sam quietly. 'I'm trying to listen. I have to find out what those Snoots are up to down there …'

What they were up to was having an argument.

'Put down that shovel, Percival,' said Margaret-Elizabeth, in as quiet a tone as her low, booming voice could go. 'It's not *time* to break through. We stick to the plan. The Roaming Scones won't be on stage until eight o'clock. Then, when they are a few songs into the show, singing about some girl or other, and the solid gold guitar is waiting at the side of the stage to be taken on for the grand finale – *that's* when we go in.' She smirked an evil smirk in the darkness – an evil, dastardly smirk that, because of the aforementioned gloom, was pretty much lost on Percival.

'Yes, dear,' he said meekly.

'Then when we have the guitar, we come back here, seal up the tunnel and lay low for a couple of weeks,' said Margaret-Elizabeth. 'And then … then we sell the guitar for MILLIONS on the internet and retire to the Canary Islands. Can you imagine it, Percival? No more beds! No more breakfasts! No more ungrateful guests! We will have smoothed down our last duvet, cleaned our last toilet, burnt our last sausage and overcharged our last guest!'

So that's why they've dug a tunnel into the Showjump Arena, thought Sam. *They want to rob the Roaming Scones' solid gold guitar!*

'Well, Tubbs,' said Sam, giving the enormous St Bernard a friendly tickle, 'we aren't going to let that happen to my favourite granny's favourite band, are we?' Tubbs wagged his tail happily. 'There's no way we're going to let those bird-brains retire to the Canaries!'

Over in O'Connell Street, Ajay was busy dealing with the other bird-brain in Sam's life, Sindy. Tourists, commuters and shoppers alike were all staring at the roof of the GPO, where Sindy was jerkily walking on her massive birdy feet from one side to the other, pecking at the stone statues of Mercury, Fidelity and Hibernia. The police below were trying to move the crowd back from the GPO's big pillars, partly for the onlookers' safety and partly because they were afraid of what would happen should the bird need to, ahem, use the bathroom. Their colleagues in the council would be cleaning up that mess for weeks!

Without warning Sindy opened her enormous blue feathery wings and fluttered down to the street, causing a backdraft that knocked several spectators over and made the GPO flags flap wildly. She landed right in front of Ajay. *Cheese and crackers*, thought Ajay, *she's almost the size of a bus!* Sindy reared up, her bird claws clicking on the street's tarmac. Now she was at her full height Ajay could see she was actually taller than the double-decker buses that were screeching to a halt in front of the GPO. She was truly gargantuan!

Sindy opened her ginormous wings again and looked like she was about to leap into the air. Ajay ran and made a leap of his own, jumping up and catching Sindy's leg as she took off and rose swiftly into the air. He clung on to her scaly leg as tightly as he could, his eyes scrunched shut. It was like hugging a tree trunk – a tree trunk that was rising into the sky, now one hundred metres up, now two hundred.

Ajay started to get cold. He opened one eye and he couldn't see cars and buses and buildings anymore, all he could see was blue sky. Then he opened his second eye and made the mistake of looking down. He could see cars and buses and buildings again – the only problem was they were all three hundred metres below him!

Sindy banked to the left with her wings spread wide, and swooped down. Ajay screeched as they narrowly missed the Dublin Spire, hoisting his legs up just in time.

Sindy changed direction again and flew in a circle over the city, her wide wings flapping lazily as she glided high up in the air. Ajay adjusted his perch on Sindy's leg and began to almost enjoy the ride. For one thing, the view was amazing – very few people had seen the city from this height. There was the Pigeon House Chimneys, there was the Samuel Beckett Bridge, there was Kilmainham Gaol. Hanging on to Sindy's massive leg with one hand, he fished around for his phone with the other.

This footage will look great on my MyTube channel, he thought. Just then Sindy made a tummy-churning turn and started to dive. *On second thoughts*, thought Ajay, *maybe I'd be better off calling Ogg about that SHRINKTASTIC stuff*.

AAAAAAAAAAAARRRRRRRRRRGGGGGGGGGGHHHHHHHHH!!

THIS IS AMY MULLIGAN ON IETV NEWS - SIZZLING NEWS THAT WON'T MAKE YOU SNOOZE.

AND NOW IN BREAKING NEWS, A GIANT BUDGIE HAS BEEN TERRORISING DOWNTOWN DUBLIN THIS EVENING. LET'S GO OVER NOW TO OUR ON-THE-SPOT REPORTER, JEMIMA VOXX-POPP, WHO IS BRAVING LIFE AND LIMB TO BRING YOU THE LATEST. JEMIMA?

JEMIMA VOXX-POPP, ON-THE-SPOT REPORTER

THANK YOU, AMY. I AM HERE IN O'CONNELL STREET, DUBLIN, A STREET THAT HAS BEEN, UP TO NOW, A PEACEFUL THOROUGHFARE, BUT THAT PEACE WAS THIS AFTERNOON SHATTERED BY WHAT CAN ONLY BE DESCRIBED AS A VERY BIG BUDGIE.

SCREEEEEEEECHHHH!!

I'VE BEEN TALKING TO SOME OF THE TERRIFIED EYEWITNESSES WHO CAME FACE TO BEAK WITH THIS GIGANTIC FEATHERY FIEND.

PAULA McARDLE, EYEWITNESS

I WAS JUST DROPPING IN TO BUY SOME STAMPS TO SEND A BIRTHDAY PRESENT TO MY GRAND-NEPHEW IN SWEDEN - HELLO, SVEN, HAPPY BIRTHDAY, LOVE ...

PAULA McARDLE, GRAND-AUNT TO SVEN

AND I WAS COMING OUT AND DIDN'T I HEAR A SQUAWKY NOISE, AND I SAYS TO MYSELF, I KNOW WHAT THAT IS, THAT'S A SQUAWK, AND DIDN'T I LOOK UP, AND DIDN'T I SEE A GREAT BIG HUGE FEATHERY THING, AND I SAYS TO MYSELF, THAT LOOKS LIKE A HUGE BIG BUDGIE, WITH THE FEATHERS AND ALL AND EVERYTHING.

PAULA McARDLE, DISAPPROVES OF GIANT BUDGIES

GREAT BIG BUDGIES, TERRORISING ME AT MY AGE? IT'S A DISGRACE, JEMIMA, A DISGRACE.

FRANK STAMP, POSTMAN

YEAH, I SAW IT - BIG BLUE YOKE. IT HOPPED DOWN ONTO THE GROUND RIGHT IN FRONT OF ME. NEARLY SQUISHED ME, IT DID.

FRANK STAMP, NEARLY SQUISHED BY BIRD

AND THEN THIS LITTLE YOUNG FELLA RAN OUTTA THE CROWD AND JUMPED ONTO ITS LEG.

FRANK STAMP, BUDGIES ARE HIS BAG

AND THEN IT TOOK OFF UP INTO THE SKY, THE YOUNG FELLA HANGIN' ON. BEEEEE-OOOTIFUL IT WAS.

POLICE WANT TO QUESTION THIS BOY...

... LAST SEEN CLINGING TO THE JUMBO BUDGIE'S LEG ...

... AS IT TOOK TO THE SKIES OVER DUBLIN.

THIS IS JEMIMA VOXX-POPP, IN DUBLIN CITY, FOR IETV NEWS.

CHAPTER SEVEN
NANNY GIGG'S SWEET TEETH

Sam sat on a kitchen chair and scratched Tubbs behind the ears. Then she scratched behind her own ears – it helped her to think. She had to stop those awful Snoots from stealing Emmaline, but how? *Hmmmm.* The best way to stop the crime from happening was to warn the Scones themselves.

'Aha! I've got it!' she cried, jumping to her feet. 'See, Tubbs,' she said to the enormous St Bernard, 'I just happen to have a special VIP meet and greet ticket, which hopefully will allow me to go backstage at the Showjump Arena, meet these Eddie and Pete characters and raise the alarm about the Snoots!'

Tubbs snuffled and looked at the tunnel.

'What's that, boy?' said Sam. 'The tunnel?' She frowned, her ginger eyebrows furrowing under her mop of curly red hair. 'Oh! I know what you're trying to say – they might try to run away and escape out of this end of the tunnel! Well, we can't have that, can we?'

Sam quickly and quietly pulled up the wooden ladder that poked out of the tunnel. She then looked around the kitchen. *What's big enough to block up this end completely?* she thought. Her eyes landed on the fridge. *That will do the job!* She unplugged it and tried to pull it out from the wall. Holy moley, it was heavy!

With much huffing and puffing she managed to get it about half a metre away from the kitchen wall. Tubbs padded over to her and licked her hand. 'Good boy,' she said softly to him, leading him around to the back of the fridge, 'you push and I'll pull, okay? All right – one, two, three!'

Between the two of them they managed to push-pull the heavy fridge to the side of the hole in the kitchen floor. Sam had a listen at the opening of the tunnel, but she couldn't hear anything. She quickly emptied the fridge, putting the contents – milk, cheese, sausages, bacon – neatly onto the kitchen table. 'Okay, Tubbs,' she said, panting a little, 'now we're going to tip this fridge over – right on top of this hole. You ready?'

The huge dog seemed to understand what he had to do. He reared up on his hind legs and joined Sam at the side of the fridge, pushing with his two furry front paws. Then Sam went to the other side of the big white domestic appliance and, using all her strength, lowered it down over the entrance to the tunnel, blocking it completely. It landed with a tiny thud. Sam held her finger to her lips. *The Snoots wouldn't have heard that, would they?*

72

Then she flew up the stairs with Tubbs running behind her. She grabbed her jacket and her VIP ticket and raced back down again. 'Okay, Tubby-baby,' she said, ruffling the brown and white fur on the big dog's head, 'we're off to meet Eddie and Pete!'

Meanwhile, over in the Showjump Arena, Eddie and Pete were leading the group of competition winners out of the green room and down several long corridors towards the stage. At least, they hoped they were going towards the stage – they got lost several times in the warren of backstage passageways. Their elderly fans, Nanny Gigg included, didn't seem to mind though, shouting 'Hello, Dublin!' at the top of their voices every time they took a wrong turn. Eventually Pete had to call their tour manager on his mobile phone to come and rescue them.

Pretty soon Nanny Gigg and the rest of the gang were sitting at the side of the stage, happily watching Eddie and Pete test the microphones and tune up their guitars.

Pete had a huge number of guitars of all shapes and sizes lined up at the side of the stage.

Some were in the shape of lightning bolts or stars, and one was a huge smiling mouth with a scone between its teeth – the Roaming Scones' logo. He went through each of them in turn, fussily twiddling the machine heads, checking the straps were on tight and generally getting them just right.

'He's a perfectionist,' Eddie told the spellbound pensioners. 'He treats each and every one of his guitars like they were his own little baby.'

'You mean he gives them rusks when they go out of tune and changes their nappies when they break a string?' asked Nanny Gigg.

Eddie threw his head back and laughed, his shiny black hair glistening in the stage lights. 'Haaawwwww hawwwwww! You're a funny one, Nanny,' he chortled, taking off his glasses and winking at her with one of his famously piercing blue eyes. Nanny Gigg felt her knees wobble and had to sit down on a big orange guitar amp to steady her nerves.

Just then there was a commotion behind the stage curtains and a flustered-looking roadie with a big silver earring appeared. 'Mister Floyd, Mister Pilchard!' cried the harried music technician.

'Richie, maaaan, we keep on telling you, the Roaming Scones touring team is a family – call us Eddie and Pete!' said Pete, looking up from his guitar.

'Sorry,' said the roadie, 'it's just there's a problem with Emmaline!'

'Emmaline?!' cried Pete, jumping quickly to his feet. 'What's wrong with my baby??'

The roadie held up a long, golden-coloured cable. 'It's her guitar lead,' he said. 'I was taking it out of the case and it just snapped!'

'The guitar lead, my dear,' said Eddie to Nanny Gigg, 'is the wire that connects an electric guitar to an amp – that's what amplifies the sound of the guitar, making it louder so the crowd can hear what's being played.'

Nanny Gigg rolled her eyes. She knew what a guitar lead was – she wasn't born yesterday. Or the day before yesterday, for that matter. 'Why don't you connect the two ends of the cable back together?' she asked the roadie. Ever practical, she was always fixing electrical bits and bobs in Hannigan's Haven. 'Wrap it in a bit of electrical tape and Bob's your Nanny! Or Bob's your Auntie, I should say – I'm the only Nanny around here!'

'Not that easy I'm afraid, missus,' said Richie the Roadie. 'The cable itself is solid gold. We'd need a good bit of gold to bridge the two broken bits.'

Pete looked hopeful. 'I'd gladly give any of my gold chains or bangles if that would help?'

'They wouldn't be thick enough,' replied Richie. 'We'd need to use two pieces of gold, and each piece would have to be at least a centimeter thick.'

Nanny Gigg raised both her arms. 'Pete, Eddie!' she cried. 'You can use my teeth!!'

The tunesome twosome looked at her as if she had suddenly sprouted an extra head, complete with a ten-gallon cowboy hat and earrings in the shape of full-sized pineapples. 'Your … teeth?' asked Pete.

'Yes,' grinned Nanny Gigg. 'My dentures are made of solid 24-karat gold!' She smiled broadly. All Eddie and Pete could see in Gigg's mouth was a pair of large white gnashers, lovely in their own way, but not exactly looking like something that was worth its weight in, well, gold.

'They're just painted white,' said Gigg. 'Daddy Mike made them for me out of solid gold and painted them white so nobody would rob them – he said they were my pension plan!' She whipped them out and scratched at a molar with one of Richie the Roadie's screwdrivers. The white coating scraped off, revealing the glittering golden colour below. 'See?' she cried triumphantly. 'Solid gold falsies!'

She handed them to Richie who, after giving them a good wipe on the front of his Crew tee-shirt, looked up at Eddie and Pete. 'They're gold all right,' he said. 'Solid 24-karat gold. They might just do the trick!'

Nanny Gigg took another set of dentures out of her handbag and slipped them into her mouth. 'It's no problem at all. I always bring a spare set of teeth, just in case.'

Richie reverently brought Emmaline onto the stage. The group of greying contest winners *ooooh*ed and *aaaaaah*ed. Richie carefully plugged one end of the broken guitar lead into Emmaline's golden socket, and plugged the other end into the biggest of the orange amps on stage. He then took Nanny Gigg's false teeth and, with a nod of the head to Nanny Gigg, held both ends of the cable together between the teeth and clamped the dentures together. 'Okay,' he said, 'that should complete the circuit – it should work now.'

'Only one way to find out, eh, Nanny Gigg?' said Pete, and he pulled Emmaline's guitar strap over his head.

'Ready?' asked Richie.

'Ready,' said Pete, and raised his bony arm high in the air.

The sound he made when his hand struck Emmaline's guitar strings was wondrous – the most melodical, beautiful chord any of the people on stage had ever heard. Several of the grown men started to weep at the sheer magnificence of the sonic vibrations emanating from the legendary solid-gold instrument. Nanny Gigg clapped her hands. 'Ah, that's brillo, Pete,' she shouted over the glorious noise. 'Give us a sing-song – how about "Girl, You Got Me in a Whirl"? I love that one!'

Eddie sat down on the amp beside Nanny Gigg. 'Well done, kid, we owe you,' he said. 'You can stick around and watch the gig from the side of the stage, if you like – the best seat in the house!'

Nanny Gigg didn't have to be asked twice.

80

81

CHAPTER EIGHT
ROCK STAR GRANNY!

Sam ran through the gates of the Showjump Arena, pushing her way past the huge crowd that was lining up behind metal barriers, waiting to be let in to see the Roaming Scones. Tubbs followed close behind, jogging cheerfully on his hefty doggy paws.

As Sam reached the door, a security guard stepped out in front of her, blocking her way. 'Woah, woah,' said the guard. 'Where do you think you're going, missy?'

Sam fished in her pocket and held up the golden VIP ticket. 'I have a ticket,' she panted. 'My granny, Nanny Gigg, is inside already!'

'Nanny Gigg is your granny?' cried the security guard. 'Well, come right this way, your dog too!' He beamed at Sam. 'Nanny Gigg is a true hero – if she hadn't sacrificed her golden gnashers the Scones would be toast! You should be very proud of her!'

'I am *always* very proud of my nanny,' said Sam, wondering what the blinkin' barnacles the burly security guard was talking about. *Sacrificed her golden gnashers??* Nanny Gigg had obviously been up to her tricks! 'Thanks, mister,' she shouted as she and Tubbs raced into the auditorium, 'and by the way, there may be twenty or thirty friends of mine following behind me!'

The vast, cavern-like auditorium was dark, lit only by the spotlights that shone on the empty stage. A few people sat in the front row, waiting for the show to begin. 'They must be the competition winners,' said Sam to Tubbs, 'but I can't see Nanny Gigg – I wonder where she is?'

She peered into the darkness, looking left and right and straining her ears for any sound of digging, but other than a low babble of excited chatter from the people in the front row she couldn't hear anything. 'Well, Tubbs,' she said to the big shaggy doggo at her side, 'it's time for you to stop being a St Bernard and start being a bloodhound – do you think you can sniff out Margaret-Elizabeth and Percival Snoot?'

Tubbs seemed to smile up at Sam, and he stuck out his tongue. He raised his snout and sniffed the air, then put his head down, snuffling and sniffling around. Without warning he scuttled quickly down one row of seats.

'Tubbs,' whispered Sam urgently, 'have you got a scent?' She cantered after the colossal canine. At the end of the row, Tubbs stopped, sniffing the air again. Then he ran back down the row of seats behind, and then he turned sharply and ran up the next one. *Where was he going?*

He came to a dead stop at a tall, black-painted wooden cube in the centre of the auditorium, the walls of which were at least two metres high. Sam could just about see an electronic desk at the top of the cube, covered in buttons and levers. 'This must be the box where they control the sound and the stage lighting for the band, Tubbs,' said Sam.

Tubbs snuffled around the wooden cube, stopping at the door. He pawed at it and whined softly.

'In here, Tubbs? Do you scent the Snoots inside here?' She turned the door handle, expecting it to be locked, but, to her surprise, the door swung open easily. *Maybe they don't lock the sound booth until the stadium is full*, thought Sam.

It was dark inside the cube, but Sam could see steps leading up to the control desk, which was on a platform about a metre off the ground. Tubbs waddled in through the door and cocked up a furry ear. From right between their feet came the unmistakable sound of metal scraping on cement. Both girl and dog stepped back and watched as a pickaxe broke through the cement floor of the sound booth, raising a huge cloud of dust.

The pickaxe head was followed by a head of dust-covered curly hair, under which was the generously proportioned body of Margaret-Elizabeth Snoot. 'You idiot, Percival,' bellowed Margaret-Elizabeth as quietly as she could, 'my hair is ruined! One's personal appearance should be tip-top when one is embarking on a solid-gold guitar heist.'

A weasel-like head with wiry grey mutton-chop sideburns popped up beside Margaret-Elizabeth. '*Koff! Koff!* Yes, dear,' he coughed in a high, flute-like voice. 'Sorry, dear.'

'Not as sorry as you're going to be!' shouted Sam. She flung open the door to the sound booth. 'They're in here, lads!' she called into the darkness of the hall. There was a loud tramping sound as thirty pairs of police boots trooped towards the booth. A gaggle of guards appeared in the doorway.

'Margaret-Elizabeth and Percival Snoot,' trumpeted the Garda Sergeant in charge, 'I am arresting you for the attempted robbery of Emmaline, the solid gold guitar belonging to my favourite band, the Roaming Scones.' He turned to the cops behind him. 'Take them away, boys!'

Two of the guards stepped over to the hole in the centre of the sound booth and hauled Percival and Margaret-Elizabeth out.

'Don't worry,' said the Sergeant, 'I think you'll find that the bed and breakfast in prison is delightful.'

'This is all your fault, Percival,' howled Margaret-Elizabeth as the guards took her and her ferret-featured husband out of the Arena. 'I never liked the Roaming Scones anyway!'

'Oh, *do* shut up, dear,' piped Percival.

'Well,' said Sam to Tubbs, 'it looks like your owners might be going for a very long holiday, just not to the Canary Islands like they planned.' She ruffled the fur on Tubbs's big, shaggy head. 'But don't worry, there's always room for one more cute, cuddly doggo in Hannigan's Haven!'

Tubbs barked happily, jumped up and licked Sam's face.

Just then, Ajay's smiling face appeared around the sound booth door, followed, not too surprisingly, by the rest of his body. A normal-sized Sindy sat on his shoulder. 'Come on, Sam,' he said, a little out of breath, 'the show's about to start!'

Sam and Ajay brought Tubbs and Sindy down to their seats in the front row. The seats around them were jam-packed with older ladies and gents, all of them wearing leather jackets, denim jeans and Roaming Scones tee-shirts, but there was no sign of Nanny Gigg. *Maybe she's in the loo*, thought Sam. *I hope she doesn't miss the start of the show …*

The lights went down, and Tubbs settled himself into Nanny Gigg's empty seat – he could hop up and sit at her feet when she got back. The Arena faded into complete blackness for a few moments, then there was an explosion of lights and noise as Eddie and Pete took to the stage and Pete rang out guitar chords from a shining red and black guitar.

The. Crowd. Went. *WILD*.

Sam and Ajay were on their feet cheering and dancing with everyone else as the Scones broke into their first number, 'Skateboard Girl'. Blue, red and green lights sparkled and spun. Pete whirled his arm on the guitar strings and Eddie whooped and wailed, singing strong and high.

'They're actually really good,' shouted Ajay over the melodic bombardment from the stage, 'you know, for two people who look like granddads!'

'Granddads and grannies are great!' shouted Sam back to Ajay. She was beginning to worry about where her granny was.

The song ended with a tumult of drums and a blazing flash of lights and the stage went dark, leaving the crowd cheering loudly. Then a spotlight picked out Eddie and Pete on the dark stage, Eddie at the microphone and Pete standing beside him with the red and black guitar.

'Hello, Dublin!' cried Eddie, pumping the air with his fist. 'Thank you for making Pete and me so welcome!'

'And now,' said Pete, 'we'd like you to welcome someone to the stage. A really good friend of ours.'

'We wouldn't be here tonight if it wasn't for this very special lady,' said Eddie.

'So we'd like you to give a good old Dublin cheer for the pride of the city, the Clobberstown Colossus … Nanny Gigg!'

A spotlight suddenly shone on a small figure to the left of Eddie and Pete. A small figure with grey curly hair, wearing an oversized Scones tee-shirt, star-shaped sunglasses, fishnet stockings and high-heeled pixie boots. A small figure holding a solid gold, jewel-encrusted guitar. Nanny Gigg took off her glasses and winked at Sam and Ajay in the front row.

The two kids' jaws dropped open in wonder as Nanny Gigg raised one arm high in the air and brought it down onto Emmaline's gold-plated guitar strings, sounding out a perfect, beautiful, resonating C chord. The drums boomed and the Roaming Scones, with Nanny Gigg on lead guitar, launched into their best-known song, 'I Wanna Love You, Girl'. Sam and Ajay stood on their seats and whooped, while Tubbs howled along in tune.

Nanny Gigg was a **Rock Star Granny!**

SHARE A STORY

From breakfast to bedtime, there's always time to discover and share stories together. You can . . .

1 TAKE A TRIP to your LOCAL BOOKSHOP

Brimming with brilliant books and helpful booksellers to share awesome reading recommendations, you can also enjoy booky events with your favourite authors and illustrators.

FIND YOUR LOCAL BOOKSHOP:
booksellers.org.uk/bookshopsearch

2 JOIN your LOCAL LIBRARY

That wonderful place where the hugest selection of books you could ever want to read awaits – and you can borrow them for FREE! Plus expert advice and fantastic free family reading events.

FIND YOUR LOCAL LIBRARY:
findmylibrary.co.uk

3 CHECK OUT the WORLD BOOK DAY WEBSITE

Looking for reading tips, advice and inspiration? There is so much for you to discover at **worldbookday.com**, packed with fun activities, games, downloads, podcasts, videos, competitions and all the latest new books galore.

SPONSORED BY

NATIONAL
BOOK
tokens

Celebrate stories. Love reading.
World Book Day is a registered charity.

WORLD
BOOK
DAY

SHARE A STORY

Well **hello** there! We are

Overjoyed that you have **joined our celebration** of

Reading books and **sharing stories**, because we

Love bringing **books** to you.

Did you know, we are a **charity** dedicated to celebrating the

Brilliance of **reading for pleasure** for everyone, everywhere?

Our mission is to help you discover **brand new stories** and

Open your mind to exciting **new worlds** and **characters**, from

Kings and **queens** to **wizards** and **pirates** to **animals** and **adventurers** and so many more. We couldn't

Do it without all the amazing **authors** and **illustrators**, booksellers and **bookshops**, publishers, schools and **libraries** out there –

And most importantly, we couldn't do it all without . . .

YOU!

On your bookmarks, get set, READ!
Happy Reading. Happy World Book Day.

Alan Nolan lives and works in Bray, County Wicklow, Ireland. He is co-creator (with Ian Whelan) of *Sancho* comic which was shortlisted for two Eagle awards, and is the author and illustrator of *The Big Break Detectives Casebook*, the 'Murder Can Be Fatal' series, *Fintan's Fifteen*, *Conor's Caveman*, *Sam Hannigan's Woof Week* and *Sam Hannigan and the Last Dodo*.

Special thanks to my brilliant editor Nicola Reddy, and to Michael O'Brien, Emma Byrne, Ivan O'Brien, all at The O'Brien Press, and to World Book Day 2019.

Extra-special thanks, as ever, to my long-suffering family, Rachel, Adam, Matthew and Sam, and to my old pals 'Steddie' Eddie Joyce and Pete 'The Roz' McClusky.

www.ALANNOLAN.ie

www.OBRIEN.ie